BULLDOGS

by Susan H. Gray

Published in the United States of America by The Child's World®
1980 Lookout Drive • Mankato, MN 56003-1705
800-599-READ • www.childsworld.com

PHOTO CREDITS
© Bob Krist/Corbis: 23
© Christine Bork/BigStockPhoto.com: 19
© Corbis: 29
© iStockphoto.com/Eric Isselée: cover, 1
© iStockphoto.com/James Pauls: 27
© Jerry Cooke/Corbis: 25
© Larry Williams/Corbis: 15, 17, 21
© Mark Raycroft/Minden Pictures: 11
© Robert Dowling/Corbis: 13
© Topical Press Agency/Stringer/Getty Images: 9

ACKNOWLEDGMENTS

The Child's World®: Mary Berendes, Publishing Director;
Katherine Stevenson, Editor

The Design Lab: Kathleen Petelinsek, Design and Page Production

LIBRARY OF CONGRESS CATALOGING-IN-PUBLICATION DATA
Gray, Susan Heinrichs.
  Bulldogs / by Susan H. Gray.
      p. cm. — (Domestic dogs)
  Includes index.
  ISBN 978-1-59296-962-3 (library bound : alk. paper)
  1. Bulldog—Juvenile literature. I. Title. II. Series.
  SF429.B85G85 2008
  636.72—dc22   2007021690

Table of Contents

NAME That DOG!

What dog is known for being stubborn? What dog looks **fierce** but is really very gentle? What dog needs its face cleaned every day? What dog is a favorite of sports teams? If you said the bulldog, you are correct!

4

5

Once Fierce, Now Gentle

No one is sure where bulldogs came from. Some people say that bulldogs' **ancestors** were mastiffs. Mastiffs are large, powerful dogs. People in England have had mastiffs for more than 2,000 years. Some people say that bulldogs' ancestors were alaunts. Alaunts were big, strong dogs, too. People kept mastiffs and alaunts as fighting and guard dogs. These big dogs were even used in war.

Great Britain is an island in Europe. It includes England, Scotland, and Wales. The map below shows where Great Britain is on Earth. The map on the right shows a closer view.

Atlantic Ocean

Scotland

North Sea

Northern Ireland

Ireland

England

Great Britain

Wales

Atlantic Ocean

English Channel

France

Bulldogs have a sad history. People used them for fighting. The dogs got their name from fighting with bulls. The dogs would bite the bulls' soft noses. The winner was the dog that held on longest. The bulls would fling the dogs about. Both the bulls and the dogs were badly hurt.

In 1835, people passed laws to stop this cruel sport. After that, fewer people wanted to own bulldogs. But some owners still liked them. They started raising them to be gentler. Over time, bulldogs changed. The dogs were no longer fighters. Today, bulldogs are known as very gentle dogs. They get along well with other animals. They are calm and friendly with children.

There are two different bulldog **breeds** today—the English Bulldog and the French Bulldog. When people just say "bulldog," they mean the English Bulldog.

This picture shows a bulldog in 1912. She was raised to be shown in dog shows instead of for fighting.

Chunky, Slobbery, Wrinkly—and Sweet

Bulldogs are chunky, heavy-set dogs. Their big bodies sit on short, strong legs. Their heads, chests, and hips are all big. But bulldogs are not tall. They are only 12 to 16 inches (30 to 41 centimeters) tall at the shoulder. Even so, they can weigh 50 pounds (23 kilograms) or more. Their coats are short and smooth. Their hair can be white, red, or tan. Some bulldogs have patches of different colors. Others have faint splotches or stripes.

You can see this bulldog's powerful legs and broad chest.

Bulldogs' faces have lots of loose skin. It hangs down around their eyes and cheeks. Their dark eyes are almost hidden by wrinkles. The wrinkles can make the dogs look worried, upset, or angry. Their big chin adds to this look. It sits far forward. The dog's lower teeth show, even when its mouth is closed. Bulldogs often look as if they are frowning!

A bulldog's nose is wide and black. The nose is flat against the dog's face. It is so flat, the dog has trouble breathing.

Bulldogs look fierce and dangerous. Their bodies are strong. Their faces look grumpy. They snort when they breathe. But these dogs are gentle, playful, and sweet.

Bulldogs have small ears for such big heads. The ears curl forward.

Does this bulldog look as if he is frowning?

The Bulldog Spirit

Bulldogs might look mean, but they are very peaceful. They are excellent family dogs. And they love attention. They are happiest when they are with their owners. They are very **loyal**. Some try to guard their families. They might even chase visitors away!

This bulldog is loved by her family.

Bulldogs sometimes have problems, too. They can be stubborn and hard to train. Sometimes they do not want to **obey** their owners. Sometimes they do not feel like learning tricks. Bulldog owners must learn how to work with this breed. It helps to starting training the dogs early. Even young puppies can learn **commands**.

Bulldogs are also known for the sounds they make. They do not bark much. But they snort and wheeze. And they snore quite loudly. Some owners find this noise comforting. But others cannot stand it!

Sometimes bulldogs sleep with their tongues hanging out. Their noses are mashed, their cheeks are floppy, and their chins stick out. These things make the dogs snore, slobber, and snort!

This bulldog has learned to balance a ball on her nose!

Bulldog Puppies

Bulldog mothers usually have four or five puppies in a **litter**. Each newborn pup weighs about 12 ounces (340 grams). This is about as heavy as a large apple.

The newborn pups have large heads. Their ears are just tiny flaps. Their eyes are tightly closed. Their faces are very wrinkled. It is hard to see their eyes!

Like all puppies, bulldog pups drink their mother's milk.

19

For the first two weeks, the puppies mostly eat and sleep. They stay close to their mother. She makes them feel warm and safe. She takes good care of them. She licks them clean. She makes sure they get enough milk.

Like other puppies, the bulldogs grow quickly. By the third week, their eyes are open. At first, bright light bothers the pups. But they soon get used to it. They look at things and begin to move around. Their mother watches them closely. She keeps them nearby. As they get older, she lets them go farther away. At three months old, they move around freely.

A month-old bulldog weighs as much as eight newborns!

Here you can see an older bulldog puppy next to an adult.

Bulldogs at Home and at Work

Today, the bulldog's main job is to be a good pet. It does this job well! That is why it is so **popular**. In 2006, it was the twelfth most popular dog in the U.S.

People think of bulldogs as tough. They think of them as never giving up. That is why many sports teams have bulldogs for **mascots**. Many schools call their sports teams Bulldogs.

This bulldog is the mascot for the University of Georgia.

Some sports teams have a real bulldog for their mascot! They dress the dog in the team colors. They bring the animal to games. Having the dog there makes the team work harder.

Yale University is a well-known school with a bulldog mascot. Its first bulldog began coming to games in 1889. The dog's name was Handsome Dan. Since then, Yale has had 15 more bulldog mascots. Every one was named Handsome Dan!

At least two American presidents had bulldogs. Warren Harding's bulldog was named Oh Boy. Calvin Coolidge's bulldog was called Boston Beans.

Here you can see 1955's Handsome Dan.

25

Caring for a Bulldog

Bulldogs look like tough animals, but they are not. In warm weather, they overheat quickly. On cool days, they get chilled. In the winter, owners often dress them in sweaters and caps.

Many bulldogs like to lie around inside. Their owners must make sure the dogs get exercise. Short walks might be all the exercise they need. Too much exercise is hard on them. Even healthy bulldogs have trouble breathing. When bulldogs exercise too much, they start gasping for air.

This happy bulldog is playing on the shore in California.

A bulldog's coat is easy to care for. The hairs are very short. They need only light brushing. The wrinkly skin is more of a problem! Dirt and bugs get trapped in the wrinkles. Owners must clean the dogs' faces and necks every day. They wipe a damp cloth between the folds of skin.

Bulldogs sometimes have eye problems. One problem is called "cherry eye." A body part that makes tears gets red and puffy. Rubbing or scratching makes it worse. **Veterinarians** can help dogs with this problem.

Bulldogs usually live to be eight to ten years old. The healthiest ones live into their teens. They make wonderful pets, but they need lots of care. In return, they give plenty of love!

Bulldogs are great pets for people in small homes. They do not need much exercise.

A veterinarian is checking this bulldog's ears for problems.

Glossary

ancestors (AN-sess-turz) Ancestors are family members who lived long ago. Bulldogs' ancestors might have been mastiffs or alaunts.

breeds (BREEDZ) Breeds are certain types of an animal. There are two breeds of bulldog.

commands (kuh-MANDZ) Commands are orders to do certain things. Bulldogs can learn to follow commands.

fierce (FEERSS) Something that is fierce is mean and dangerous. Bulldogs look fierce, but they are not.

litter (LIH-tur) A litter is a group of babies born to one animal. Bulldog litters often have four or five puppies.

loyal (LOY-ul) To be loyal is to be true to something and stand up for it. Bulldogs are loyal to their owners.

mascots (MASS-kots) Mascots are things people think bring good luck to a team. Some sports teams have bulldogs as mascots.

obey (oh-BAY) To obey someone is to do what the person says. Sometimes bulldogs do not obey their owners.

popular (PAH-pyuh-lur) When something is popular, it is liked by lots of people. Bulldogs are popular.

veterinarians (vet-rih-NAIR-ee-unz) Veterinarians are doctors who take care of animals. Veterinarians are often called "vets" for short.

To Find Out More

Books to Read

American Kennel Club. *The Complete Dog Book for Kids.* New York: Howell Book House, 1996.

Fiedler, Julie. *Bulldogs.* New York: PowerKids Press, 2006.

Frisch, Joy. *Bulldogs.* North Mankato, MN: Smart Apple Media, 2004.

Stone, Lynn M. *Bulldogs.* Vero Beach, FL: Rourke Publishing, 2007.

Places to Contact

American Kennel Club (AKC) Headquarters
260 Madison Ave, New York, NY 10016
Telephone: 212-696-8200

On the Web

Visit our Web site for lots of links about bulldogs:

http://www.childsworld.com/links

Note to Parents, Teachers, and Librarians: We routinely check our Web links to make sure they're safe, active sites—so encourage your readers to check them out!

Index

About the Author

Susan H. Gray has a Master's degree in zoology. She has written more than 70 science and reference books for children. She loves to garden and play the piano. Susan lives in Cabot, Arkansas, with her husband Michael and many pets.